THE ADVENTURES
VICK BICK
THE LIFE OF AN INK PEN

Suzanne Coffey Mielke
Illustrated by Artisticco

LifeRich Publishing is a registered trademark of The Reader's Digest Association, Inc.

LifeRich Publishing books may be ordered through booksellers or by contacting:

LifeRich Publishing
1663 Liberty Drive
Bloomington, IN 47403
www.liferichpublishing.com
1 (888) 238-8637

Because of the dynamic nature of the Internet, any web addresses or links contained in this book may have changed since publication and may no longer be valid. The views expressed in this work are solely those of the author and do not necessarily reflect the views of the publisher, and the publisher hereby disclaims any responsibility for them.

All Illustrations by Artisticco

ISBN: 978-1-4897-2951-4 (sc)
ISBN: 978-1-4897-2952-1 (hc)
ISBN: 978-1-4897-2950-7 (e)

Print information available on the last page.

LifeRich Publishing rev. date: 07/01/2020

Special Thanks

Caroline Mielke
Cecelia Andon
David Coffey

Carole Gruber
Mai Coffey

Dedicated to my grandchildren,

Levi Charles Crenshaw
Mayes Holland Crenshaw
Asher Matthew Crenshaw

Owen Joel Crenshaw
Samuel James Mielke
Noah Anne Mielke

my children and their spouses,

Matthew Charles Mielke
Caroline Elizabeth Mielke

Meredith Mielke Crenshaw
Charles Ligon Crenshaw IV

and my nieces and nephews,

Hunter Rushing Johnson
Peter Joseph Johnson
Parker Charles Johnson
Mary Elizabeth Johnson
Charles Michael Coffey

Alexandra Nikita Coffey
Emily Coffey Feldbruegge
Wyatt Douglas Feldbruegge
Kathleen Mai Coffey
Kristi Lee Hepner

CONTENTS

The Characters List

Vick Bick

Brigitte
French Postcard

Matt

Cecil
The Giant Eraser

Meredith

Bob

Vicky

Max

Sally

Mayor
William White Out

Hilary

Hunter

Parker

Rubber Band

Emily

Kat

Solar Calculator

Mary Elizabeth

Red Marker

Pete

Flash Light

Allie

Paper Clip

Kristi

Sticky Pad

Charlie

The Hole Punch

Owen
Duct Tape

Levi
Laser Pointer

Mayes
Mini First Aid Kit

Wyatt
Tape

Samuel
Sunglasses

Mr. Chas Bick

Noah
Lost Key

Caroline
The Feather Pen

Asher
Compass

INTRODUCTION

Have you ever noticed that ink pens end up having no specific owner? There are people who try to hold on to a certain ink pen, but eventually their efforts fail. The people lend the pens to someone or lose them, and others pick the pens up. Pens circulate through life as though they are the property of the universe, passing from one person to another. Have you ever thought about the travels of an ink pen, or should I say, the life of an ink pen?

CHAPTER 1

THE BIRTH OF VICK BICK

It was a warm day in Clearwater, Florida, and Bob Smith went to work. He was an inventory control supervisor in the Bick pen factory, and his job was to make sure no defective pens left the plant. It was a boring, tedious job, but it provided a good income, so Bob committed himself to the job and did it with much joy.

On that particular day, Bob was sitting at the conveyer belt, waiting for the first pens to appear. Production began, and the first pen rolled out. Bob saw that the word *Vick* was imprinted on the pen instead of *Bick*. He shouted, "Stop the printing now!" He snatched up the pen, and instead of throwing it in the trash, as he usually did with other defective pens, he put it in a special case, complete with an ink refill cartridge.

No, this pen is unique, he thought. *In all the years that I have worked here, I have never witnessed a misprint*. The misprint resulted in the birth of Vick Bick. Bob told a fellow worker, "Instead of throwing it away because it's different, I want to give this special pen to my girlfriend, Vicky. She will watch over it and take good care of it."

Now the other Bick pens were watching from a box on the shelf labeled "Perfect Pens." They were ready to be sent to some of the most famous retail stores in the world. They heard the conversation and laughed.

"Now what does that man want with a messed-up pen? It should be discarded immediately," said Bick #4459.

Another Bick pen said, "Since he won't be put in a store, no one will know he exists."

"We should all remain quiet and let him go home with the man," said another one.

"Well, you have a point," said Bick #4459.

"Let him go. I feel sorry for him. He'll end up in the trash sooner or later," replied another pen.

Meanwhile, at Bob's girlfriend's house, there was a lot of noise coming out of a desk drawer. Vicky had passed her desk in a hurry several times that morning while getting ready for work. Her television was on, and she was listening to the news. The newscast drowned out the noise from the drawer, so she was unaware of what was going on inside of it.

Soon she was dressed and left for work. Little did she know there was a whole world that existed inside that drawer.

CHAPTER 2

THE PARADE

That night, as Vicky slept, conversation between the office supplies could be heard coming from the drawer. The mayor of Desk Drawer City said, "I command that the celebration parade begin!" The mayor was Mr. William White Out, who was a very punctual mayor. City events always had to start on time, and he wanted no mistakes.

The parade began with a splash of color. First came a smart-looking formation of highlighters, whose job was to highlight the parade route. They highlighted it in yellow, green, and orange. The route looked very well planned as well as colorful. Meredith, the ruler, followed the highlighters, measuring the parade route. She always insisted that everything that went on in the city be recorded with perfect measurements. She kept every measurement recorded in the desk journal, which was why Hilary, the desk journal, followed her so closely, observing every measurement.

Finally, it was time for the big float to come along the parade route. It was Matt, the stapler! He moved very slowly and with great poise. The multicolored stapler certainly stood out in the parade, as he did every day because of his beautiful coloring. Next in line were the paper clips. They were dancing in perfect unison and playing trumpets, trombones, and drums. They were followed by an array of colorful magic markers doing cartwheels, flips, and somersaults. Following the markers were two rolls of Scotch tape. Being of Scottish descent, they played the bagpipes.

The Bick army ink pens marched along next, followed by the #2 air force pencils. The city had its own defense system in place, even though there had not been a reason for it. Because of the advancement in technology and the invasion of laptops, Desk Drawer City had remained quiet for the past five years. The desk drawer was rarely opened, and the supplies were hardly ever used.

Cecil, the giant eraser, came along next. She kept shouting, "Ouch!" because the thumbtacks had attached themselves to her so that they could ride in the parade. As she moved, a tack would fall off. When a tack fell off the eraser float, he would run and jump back on her again. This was fun for the tacks—they would laugh and giggle—but for Cecil it hurt. As a result, "Ouch!" became the song that accompanied this float. Cecil would stroll down the parade route singing, and the words to the song were easy to remember: "Ouch! Ouch! Ouch! Ouch! Ouch!" Everyone sang the "Ouch!" song as the float passed. It was a funny sight to see, and the drawer was filled with laughter.

Kat, the pocket calculator, was part of Cecil's float debut. She was walking behind Cecil, adding up the number of times Cecil was stuck with a tack. Kat turned the scene into a game. As they walked, she would display a number to the audience. The number being displayed was the number of times the eraser had been stuck. Everyone would giggle and laugh.

Charlie, the hole punch, followed behind Cecil and Kat. All the misplacements were riding on top of Charlie. This included the nail polish, the hair clip, a roll of string, lipstick, eye shadow, tweezers, a small hammer, and a small screwdriver. They were referred to as "the misplacements" because they were in the wrong drawer.

The parade ended with the rubber bands. They would shoot up in the air and fall down, as though they were skydivers. They never got hurt doing this stunt because of their flexibility. The parade was followed by a dance. It was quite a sight to see.

Once the parade ended, all the desk drawer contents swirled around to the music. After the first song ended, a country song began playing. The rubber bands and the small eraser tops took over the dance floor to perform. The rubber bands rode the small erasers tops as if they were in a rodeo. They did this to the beat of the music, and there was a lot of whooping and hollering. After the performance, Mr. White Out stood up to give a speech.

"Quiet, everyone!" shouted Matt, the stapler.

"Ladies and gentlemen, as mayor of Desk Drawer City, I think it is important that we go over the safety rules of our city. I think we are becoming a bit lax. I know we have not had any activity in this drawer for five years, but you never know when something could happen.

"Remember, when we are in the presence of humans, we cannot move or speak. When the desk drawer is open, there must be total stillness and silence. We should only move around at nighttime, after Vicky has gone to sleep, unless there is an extreme emergency.

"I have also been concerned about the noise level in here because our day needs to end before Vicky wakes up. I know she thinks it's her television, but how long can we hide behind that noise? If she ever figures out it is not her television, we could all be cleaned out and thrown away. Please remain vigilant and dedicated. I would hate to see our city go into the trash. We do not want to be cleaned out."

Everyone knew the mayor was right, so they all agreed to be more careful. Committees were formed to study the weaknesses in their defense system.

Finally, daylight came, and the drawer contents went to sleep. They always tried to sleep during the day, so they would not get the attention of Vicky.

"THE PARADE CONTINUES"

CHAPTER 3

THE GIFT

It was later that evening that Bob stopped by to give Vicky the ink pen. "How wonderful!" she exclaimed. "I love the case that the pen comes in!" As she opened it, she giggled. "Look—it's a misprint. I love his name because it's similar to mine!"

Bob said, "That's why I saved him from being thrown in the trash."

"The refill cartridge will come in handy as well," she stated. "I will be the only woman with a Vick Bick pen!"

Vicky hugged Bob and ran upstairs to her office. She opened the desk drawer and threw in the cased ink pen. She closed the drawer and went back downstairs.

Vicky and Bob left to go out to dinner.

It was dark inside the desk drawer. The only light that could be detected was from the light of many eyes moving back and forth. There was about five minutes of total silence.

Pete, the flashlight, turned on and illuminated the entire drawer. The contents of the drawer came alive. Parker, the thickest rubber band, exclaimed, "Thanks, Pete! I don't know what we would do without you. We would never be able to see around this dark drawer if it weren't for you."

There was much hustle, bustle, and commotion as everyone surrounded the ink-pen case. The topic of conversation became whether they should open the case.

"It could be an alien ink pen that could destroy us," shouted one of the pens.

"I vote no," yelled Hunter, a #2 pencil.

Just then, Mayor White Out approached the case. "I summon all those who are on the Package Opening Committee to step forward. We will let them decide whether the case should be opened. Are all the members here?" asked the mayor.

The reinforcements stepped forward, as they were part of the committee. They were the ones used to reinforce the holes that Charlie the hole punch made. "We are here," they shouted.

The other members of the Desk Drawer Committee moved forward as well. Cecil, the eraser, stepped forward and said, "An alien invasion is my guess!"

A group of paper clips led by Allie, the largest paper clip and pink in color, formed a paper clip chain and moved forward. "We are prepared to do what it takes to make sure our city is safe," said Allie.

Meredith, the ruler, moved forward. "I am prepared to make a ruling in this case." She began to measure the size of the case, since she wanted to determine exactly the number of pens that could fit inside the fancy case. "My guess is that there are two alien pens inside, and I don't think more than that could fit," she said.

Mary Elizabeth, the red magic marker, moved forward and said, "I vote not to open it. By the unusual markings on the case, I say the ink pens are from France."

"Who speaks French?" shouted the mayor. No one responded because all the drawer contents had been made in the "Good old USA."

"No foreign imports here!" shouted Emily, the glue.

Suddenly, a pretty postcard from France stepped forward. She had arrived the day before, and Vicky had put her in the desk drawer early in the morning when everyone was sleeping.

"I speak French," said the postcard as everyone turned and looked at her. "My name is Brigitte."

"When did you get here?" asked Hunter, the #1 pencil.

"Early this morning, while you all were still asleep," replied Brigitte. "I hope you don't mind, but it looks like I will be here awhile."

Well, all the pens and pencils went googly-eyed over her; she was beautiful.

The pens and pencils tripped over themselves and stumbled on their words. "Of course not—stay as long as you like," they said.

Mayor White Out looked at Brigitte and said, "I hope you weren't offended by Emily's last remark."

Brigitte replied, "No, monsieur, I understand the pride you have for your country. We have the same pride in France. I am a bit embarrassed because I have no words written on me. French postcards should have words of love on them. I do not have a romantic message of any sort. Being French, it is usual to have a romantic message. Maybe while I am here, I can get some words added and find some stamps to help me get back to France."

All the ink pens eagerly replied, "I think that can be arranged."

"Oh by the way, looking at the case, it is not from France," Brigitte replied.

Suddenly Matt, the multicolored stapler, who was one of the most respected tools in the drawer, emerged. He strolled quietly toward the case; everyone remained quiet, waiting to see what he would say. Matt had the ability to put together any torn page with one click or staple together special projects. This was a big deal to everyone because his ability made him a respected leader in the city.

Just as Matt began to speak, pounding started coming from the pen case. A shout of "Let me out of here!" was heard. Everyone gasped and jumped back from the pen case.

Parker, the giant rubber band, shouted, "Don't let him out! He could be from outer space!"

"Don't be silly," said Matt. "There are no pen manufacturers in space!"

Mary Elizabeth, the red marker, moved forward and said, "Well, you could be wrong. Anything is possible."

"You have been reading way too many comic books," said Matt.

Matt instructed everyone to help him turn the case over. Printed on the bottom of the case were the words "Made in the USA, in the great state of Florida."

Matt said, "Looks like what we have here is not foreign at all."

Another shout emerged from the case: "Get me out of here! I am not a foreigner!"

Matt shouted back at the case, "Please identify yourself and your partner."

The voice shouted back, "It's just me, Vick Bick, and my refill cartridge. Now please let me out; it's dark in here!"

"A what?" asked Kat, the pocket calculator. "What in the world is a Vick Bick?" She began laughing, and everyone joined in.

Parker, the rubber band, said, "It sounds like a misprint to me."

Emily, the glue, exclaimed, "I am not sure what is going on, but this could become a very sticky situation."

With this being said, Meredith, the ruler, stepped forward. "I rule that we let him out. My measurements do seem to confirm that what he is telling us is true."

The Opening Committee huddled together in a deep discussion.

Mayor White Out was losing his patience and asked them, "Have you reached a decision yet?"

Matt, the stapler, said, "Yes, we have."

"What is your decision?" asked Mayor White Out.

"We have decided that we should open the case," responded Matt.

"Do you have a plan on how to do this?" asked the mayor.

"Yes, I believe we do," Matt answered.

"Okay, move forward with the plan," said Mayor White Out.

The tweezers stepped up to pick the lock. Allie, the large paper clip, and the rest of the paper clips formed a paper clip chain.

Allie attached herself to the picked lock and shouted to the other paper clips, "Pull!"

Matt grabbed the chain and began pulling the paper clip chain and yelled to Vick Bick, "Now push!"

Inside the case Vick had tipped himself slightly upward by resting on the ink refill cartridge. Using this leverage, he pushed the case with all of his might.

The case popped open.

Vick shouted, "Thank you! I thought I never would get out of there."

All the contents of the drawer gathered around Vick and stared. They had never seen a misprint before.

Chas, the largest Bick ink pen in the drawer, rolled forward and asked, "What happened to you? Shouldn't you be a Bick?"

Vick looked down shyly and replied, "Yes. I was born this way. I was supposed to be thrown in the trash, ground up, and recycled, but a kind man saved my life and brought me here."

They all began to tease him about his imprint being wrong and sadness overcame him.

"I cannot help the way I was made," Vick replied.

Matt scooted up close to Vick and took a protective stance.

"Now, everyone, leave him alone, or I'll staple you all to the side of the drawer! No one is perfect because we are all made by machinery that man invented. Now, Mr. Chas Bick, did you ever notice that you have a dent in your back? Well of course not—how could you? You have no eyes on the back of your cap! And, Kat, your calculating services are not always accurate. Parker, one part of your rubber band is smaller than the other side. Need I go on?"

Everyone looked down at the ground in remorse.

"You are right. We are so sorry for judging you by your appearance," they all said in unison.

Kat said, "We immediately judged you on your misprint, but we need to look at your heart instead. We indeed are very sorry."

A voice was heard coming from the back. It was Brigitte, the French postcard. "Yes, it is the heart that matters," she said as she smiled and looked at Vick. She continued, "Bonjour! I am Brigitte, and I am new here too. I arrived yesterday from France. I am a postcard with no words, so I am different compared with other French postcards. You are not the only one who is new and different."

The minute Vick saw Brigitte, his thoughts turned to love and romance. By the look in her eyes, it was mutual. It appeared to be love at first sight between the two of them.

Everyone gathered around Brigitte and Vick, telling them about their lives. They told Vick and Brigitte that they had been in the desk drawer for five years, with no activity.

"We have not been used once," said Meredith, the ruler. "The only ruling I get to do is to rule on the laws of Desk Drawer City. That is not the kind of ruling I was made to do. You know, I would like to actually measure something."

Hunter, the #2 pencil, said, "I have never even been sharpened, so I have no point." He looked down at the ground as he spoke.

Charlie, the hole punch, said, "Look inside. I have no paper circles in my paper holder. I have punched nothing in years, and my tray is empty."

Parker, the rubber band, said, "I have bound nothing!"

Allie, the giant pink paper clip, said, "And I have clipped nothing!"

Emily, the glue, said, "Yes, I have not stuck anything together in years."

Kat, the calculator, said, "That's why my calculations are off, I haven't been practicing my math enough. Being solar powered doesn't help matters either."

Mary Elizabeth, the red marker, said, "My ink is drying up because of a lack of use."

Kristi, the sticky note pad, said, "My stickiness is rapidly drying up. Eventually I will need assistance from Wyatt, the Scotch tape, to post my notes."

Even Mayor White Out chimed in. "I have not corrected anything in years."

Pete, the flashlight, said, "Well, I guess I am in a different situation. I am used every day for light, so I feel complete, happy, and useful. To sum things up, you all complete me!"

Everyone giggled.

Mary Elizabeth asked, "Isn't that a line out of a famous movie?"

Matt, the stapler, said, "Now everything you all are saying is true. I haven't been used either, but let's look on the bright side. We have not been thrown away in the trash, borrowed, or lost in the world. We have all been safe in this drawer."

It seemed that the arrival of Vick Bick and Brigitte had brought excitement back to the supply drawer. Vick Bick brought encouragement to the supplies and even made them look forward to the future again.

CHAPTER 4

LIVING IN DESK DRAWER CITY

Life in Desk Drawer City was extremely satisfying to Vick Bick for the first three weeks. He spent his time helping others accomplish things, and in turn this made them feel useful. After all, that is what everyone really wanted in this world. Everyone wanted to feel needed, loved, and useful. They needed a reason to live and a way to contribute to making the world a better place.

The laptop computer that was sitting on the desktop could hear everything that was going on inside the drawer and became a little irritated; he believed he was the wave of the future and the supplies were worthless. He resented them being so happy and cheerful. He never thought about the fact that, with all the advances being made in technology, over time he could be considered outdated and useless too.

The laptop listened as Vick Bick held up Hunter, the #2 pencil, to a small handheld sharpener. With the help of other supplies, Vick helped spin the pencil in the sharpener and finally gave Hunter a point. Everyone cheered, and Vick Bick said, "Now look what we can accomplish if we work as a team."

Vick Bick next had Mary Elizabeth, the red marker, in charge of decorating the drawer walls with artwork. She had all the supplies working on this project, and they even held an art contest. Matt, the stapler, helped hang the artwork on the walls of the drawer. Vick, admiring all the artwork, said, "Isn't it fun making your surroundings beautiful?"

Vick also spent time encouraging the supplies to filter paper into Charlie, the hole punch, in order to fill his paper tray with paper circles. The opening and closing of the hole punch became a routine morning workout. The opening and closing sound reminded everyone of someone lifting a weight and then putting it down, since Charlie would moan and groan every time he punched holes. Eventually, as the weeks passed, Charlie felt fit and was very grateful. Vick exclaimed, "It is very important for everyone to stay physically fit. Look how strong Charlie has become."

Kristi, the sticky note pad, was now being used to post notes of encouragement around the desk drawer. Vick wrote a note on her pad and posted it for all to see: "Today is going to be a great day!"

There were many other things Vick Bick contributed to in the desk drawer, and everyone was very happy. Everyone came to love Vick Bick because he was so thoughtful and tried to help everyone all the time.

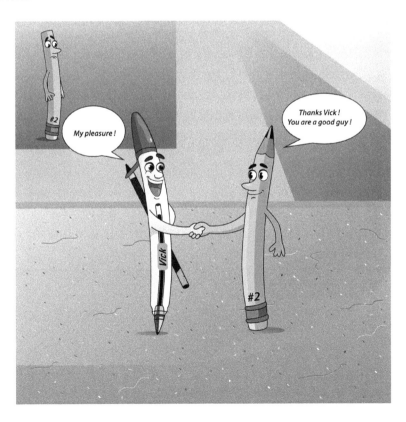

CHAPTER 5

VICK QUESTIONS HIS LIFE

After several weeks, Vick found himself questioning things. "How can you stand not being used by people? I have thought about this situation for many weeks, and I just think it is an awful way to live."

"Well it sure beats getting used up and thrown away in the trash," said Mr. Chas Bick, the giant Bick pen. "I remember back in the days when we were being used a lot, many pens went missing. When a pen or pencil was removed from our city, they never came back. They usually ended up lost in the world forever. We have never known of any of them to make it back! As a matter of fact, we really don't know what happens to them. All we know is that if you leave here, you never come back."

Vick replied, "I am a young pen, and I am not ready to just sit in a drawer for the rest of my life. I need a purpose, a reason to be a pen. No, just sitting in drawer will not happen to me. I want to travel and see the world. I want to lead the life of a pen. I would rather lead a short life full of adventure than just remain captive in a drawer for the rest of my life."

"Well good luck with that!" shouted Cecil, the giant eraser. "The drawer is never open, so how can you possibly get out?"

"Hmm, that is a good point," said Meredith, the ruler.

CHAPTER 6

ASKING FOR HELP

The next day Vick gathered Mayor White Out and all the supplies together. He said to all of them, "I have to get out of this drawer. I don't want to live and not be used. I need a plan, and I am going to need everyone's help coming up with one. I have to get out of here. Please, can you all help me?" Just as he finished his sentence, a young laser pointer named Levi approached him.

"Hi, I am a laser pointer. I know that I'm young, but I am extremely eager to learn. Can I go with you if you decide to get out of here? I would help you on your adventure, pointing out the way that you need to go. I could also distract cats and dogs if they start to bother you."

The others began to plead their case for going on the adventure with Vick. Mayes, a small first aid kit, strolled up and said, "I would like to go too. There is a great chance that you could be injured on your mission, and I could be there to help repair your boo-boos."

Just then Charlie laughed and said, "Isn't that what Brigitte is for, to kiss his boo-boos?"

Everyone began to giggle, and Brigette and Vick blushed.

Asher, a pocket compass, said, "Take me! I can help you find your way in this very large world. I can show you the direction that you need to go. It's important that I help others find their way in life."

Samuel, a pair of sunglasses, said, "Take me! I can be your eyes."

19

Everyone laughed, and shouted, "Vick already has eyes!"

Samuel replied, "That's a nickname given to me, since I help people see what's really out there. What I mean is, I can shield your eyes when the sun is too bright and you cannot see. I have another useful talent too: I come equipped with night vision shades, so when it is dark outside, I can help you see in the dark."

Noah, a key, said, "I am the one that really needs to go. I am a key with no keyhole. I don't know what I open, and that mystery needs to be revealed. I could be the key to a very important drawer or door that could help you."

Last, but not least, Owen, a roll of duct tape, said, "As a spokesman for duct tape, I can assure you that I can help fix things and hold things together that could be very useful for your trip. I can do just about anything."

Vick said, "Hold on. While I sympathize with each of you and your reasons for wanting to go, I need to travel solo this time. You heard everyone: chances are I may not make it back to the drawer. I don't want to put anyone in danger until I learn the ropes of exploration. Besides, if we all go at once, it would draw too much attention. Maybe we can work that out in the future, if I make it back."

Everyone walked away. They were sad and disappointed, but they all knew Vick was right.

Mayor White Out said, "I think we should help Vick if he wants to go. If he makes it back, he would be able to answer a lot of questions for us about the outside world."

The mayor turned to Vick and said, "You know you only have so much ink and when you run out of it you will be thrown away in the trash."

"I am well aware of the risk. I will take my refill with me," said Vick.

At that very moment Sally, Vicky's cat, jumped on the desk and began prancing around.

"Everyone, quiet!" shouted the Mayor. "It's that cat again." Everything in the desk drawer shook as if there was an earthquake. All the office supplies started shifting, and everyone ran for cover.

Cecil, the eraser, shouted to the pens, "Keep your tops on, and hold on!"

Finally Sally jumped off the desk, and the shaking stopped.

"That was a close one," said Meredith.

Mayor White Out began to speak again. "Now, as I was saying, I think we need to help Vick Bick get out of here."

CHAPTER 7

THE PLAN

From the crowd, a voice was heard, "I think I have an idea."

Everyone turned to the direction of the voice, but no one could see who was speaking.

The mayor shouted, "Whoever said that, please come forward."

The crowd of supplies parted, and out walked Caroline, a feather ink pen.

The mayor said, "Okay, what is your idea?"

"Well, we can use my feather to lure the cat to open the drawer."

Mayor White Out said, "That is much too risky! The cat has the ability to do a lot of damage playing with everyone—not to mention chewing on us and dragging us across the floor."

Mary Elizabeth, the magic marker, spoke up with a suggestion. "I have an idea. What if we make a lot of noise so that the lady will open up the drawer. We will have Vick Bick propped up, ready to leave. We could write a note and attach it to him. The note would simply say, 'Vicky, please take me out of this drawer and use me. I want to have a purpose for my life. I need an adventure. Your friend, Vick Bick.'"

"I think that might freak her out," said the mayor.

Charlie, the hole punch, spoke up. "Why don't we get everyone in the drawer to run at the

23

drawer all at once and bang on it until it opens? All we need is to make a large enough crack for Vick to get out. Parker and a couple of the other rubber bands could form a sling shot and shoot Vick out like a rocket!"

Vick said, "Ouch. I could lose my top, or I could be slammed up against a wall and broken. No, that does not sound very safe to me."

"Quiet!" yelled Mayor White Out. "Vicky is coming."

It was morning, and Vicky was on her way to work. The phone rang, and she picked up the phone and said, "Okay, I will stop by today to sign the car loan papers." She hung up the phone and mumbled to herself, "I need to remember to take a pen today." Everyone in the drawer got quiet, scurried into place, and quickly laid down.

"Quiet!" the Mayor shouted, "Don't move!"

The mayor said to Vick, "This might be your lucky day. Get ready to go. I bet that at any moment she will open this drawer to get a pen. If you stick out enough, I guarantee that she will pick you."

Wyatt, the Scotch tape, moved quickly forward to tape Vick's refill to his back. The other pens then propped Vick up in the middle of the drawer, making him an obvious pick. Everyone got quiet and waited. The only thing moving was Vick's eyes, back and forth. He could feel his heart racing.

Brigitte, the French postcard, said, "We just met. Do you really have to go? I am afraid I won't see you again."

Vick replied, "I will be back. I was made for adventure. I just cannot stay in this desk drawer for the rest of my life. Will you wait for me?"

Brigitte batted her long lashes. "Maybe," she said with a smile.

They could hear Vicky walking around the house. They could hear her take a shower and then got dressed. It sounded like she was almost ready to leave.

Vicky passed by the desk and plopped her purse down on top of it, without opening the drawer.

Matt, the stapler, said, "Well, she sure is taking her sweet time. She must already have a pen in her purse."

Caroline, the feather pen, spoke up again. "Let me lure the cat to open the drawer. And then the paper clips can form a ladder for Vick to use to climb out. Once he is on top of the desk, he can run and get in her purse."

Allie, the giant paper clip, said, "I will be happy to direct all my fellow clips in the plan."

The mayor said, "But the cat is extremely dangerous."

Caroline replied, "There is a simple solution, and it involves timing. Remember the lady always feeds the cat right before she leaves for work. If we time this right, the drawer could be opened at the exact minute that the cat will be called for breakfast. Sally won't turn down any opportunity to eat! Vick can climb out of the drawer and get in her purse. When she returns to get her purse, she will see that the drawer is open and close it."

"Well that is quite an impressive plan coming from a feather pen," said the mayor.

Matt said, "I say let's go for it."

"It sounds good to me," said Meredith, the ruler.

The Mayor turned to everyone and shouted, "All in favor of the plan say, 'Aye.'"

Everyone responded, "Aye!

CHAPTER 8

THE ESCAPE

"Okay, we need to move fast. Vick, I want to wish you all the best. I hope you have a very adventuresome life and that you don't get lost," said the mayor. "Make sure you look both ways before you cross the street. If you ever need help, find a police officer, and he will help you. Be respectful to those in authority, and follow their instructions. Always follow the law. Be polite and kind to others, and always show them unconditional love. Avoid people who are involved in crime of any sort. And last, but not least, always keep plenty of ink with you.

"Now let's get started with the plan. Everyone, assume your positions," shouted the mayor.

Everyone heard the cat walking around the room. The paper clips formed a ladder for the feather pen to climb up. The sticky pads volunteered to form a hammock, so if the feather pen fell, she would have a soft landing.

The feather pen climbed up the paper clip ladder and began moving her feather back and forth through the crack in the drawer. Everyone heard the cat running toward the drawer.

"Brace yourselves!" yelled the mayor. The cat pounced up on top of the desk and began clawing at the drawer. The feather pen kept teasing the cat. With each motion, the drawer would open a little bit.

"One more swipe and the drawer should be open enough for Vick to get out," said Matt, the stapler.

"Everyone, prepare to take cover!" shouted Meredith, the ruler.

The next thing they knew, the drawer opened, the feather pen jumped into the hammock, and the cat began dangling his paw down in the drawer. Just as he began clawing and swiping at everything, Vicky shouted, "Sally! Here kitty, kitty. It's time to eat."

The cat reared up his head and looked over his shoulder.

Vicky called again, "Sally! Here kitty, kitty! If you don't come now, you will not get anything to eat until this evening."

That was all the encouragement the cat needed. She jumped off the desk and ran into the kitchen.

"Yeah!" shouted everyone. "It worked!"

"Congratulations on a job well done," said Mayor White Out.

Matt, the stapler, said, "Vick, you need to move fast; I hear the lady coming."

Vick scurried up the ladder and started making a mad dash to the purse. Everyone in the drawer held their breath and remained motionless.

What everyone did not take into consideration was Max, the laptop computer. He was awake on top of the desk and doing some online shopping. When he saw Vick running across the desk, he shouted, "Who goes there? What is your username and the password? You cannot just get on my desk; you have to submit a written request several days in advance to be up here. All approvals must come from me. I have a good mind to give you a virus!"

Vick replied, "I am getting out of here now, so you will not be bothered with me."

"Please be quiet while I analyze the data you just presented to me," replied Max. He then typed into the search engine "What are the chances that an ink pen will make it back to their desk drawer?" The answer came back, saying "less than 3 percent."

Max thought for a moment and then said, "Okay, I'll let you go this time without the appropriate documentation, but from now on, you have to fill out the legal paper work. Do you understand?" He raised his eyebrows as he questioned Vick.

"Yes, sir," replied Vick. "Please thank your operating system for me."

"Okay, but you better get going!" said Max. "Those pens and pencils are useless," he mumbled under his breath.

Just as Vicky entered the room, Vick fell down and remained totally still. He was right next to her purse but he had not made it inside.

Vicky grabbed her purse and started digging around in it, mumbling, "Where is my pen?" She looked down and saw Vick lying on the table. "Oh, there it is. It must have fallen out of my purse." She picked up the pen. She put Vick in her purse and then reached over and closed the drawer.

Everyone could hear her walking away, and then they heard the door open and close as she left for work. She was now on her way to the bank with Vick.

Every item in the desk drawer cheered: "We did it!"

CHAPTER 9

THE ADVENTURE BEGINS

Vick was lying motionless in Vicky's purse. The only things moving were Vick's eyes. They moved back and forth in a rapid movement. As he looked around inside the purse, he saw another pen hiding behind the Kleenex. It was a Bick, #202 to be exact.

Vick whispered to the other pen. "Hey, my name is Vick. It is nice to meet you."

The other pen replied, "I am Chris, Bick ID #202. It is nice to meet you too."

"Would you mind if the lady picks me to sign the car loan papers?" asked Vick. "I am ready for an adventure."

The Bick pen replied, "Not at all. It would be a welcome relief. My ink is only half full, and my time is running out. So please feel free to take over this task."

Vick said, "When the lady opens her purse, you need to hide in the bottom. I will place myself toward the top of the bag, in an obvious position, so that she will grab me instead of you. How does that sound?"

"Great," replied the Bick pen. "But you do know that when you leave there is always a chance that you won't return. You could be lost or misplaced forever!"

"Yes, I do," said Vick. "That is a chance that I am willing to take. Life is full of risks, and sometimes you have to take a chance in order to accomplish some wonderful things. You simply cannot let fear keep you from trying something new. I will feel that I wasted my life if I don't venture out into the world."

"Interesting concept," replied Chris Bick #202. "I personally am just trying to stay alive by not running out of ink. What you are saying is very, very risky. The more you do, the greater the chances are of you running out of ink and landing in the trash, and who knows where you'll end up then. No one knows where the trash goes."

"Okay, understood," said Vick. "I still want to sign those car loan papers. Are we in agreement?"

Chris agreed to the plan.

The pens assumed their positions in the purse. Vick stood on top of a candy bar, so the lady would see him, and Chris hid behind the reading glasses in the bottom of the handbag. They heard the lady drive into the bank parking lot and stop the car. They heard the door open, and then Vicky picked up her purse.

Chris whispered to Vick. "Hold on—the purse contents are going to shift!"

Everything happened so fast that Vick did not have time to respond to Chris. A penny fell and hit Vick in the head, followed by a breath mint. "Ouch!" he said.

"I warned you," said Chris. "This always happens when Vicky picks up her purse. Now hold on tight until she puts her purse down."

Vick said, "I am so excited. I get to sign car loan documents today. This is going to be a great day. I get to be a part of helping someone get a new car. I was made to help others. Besides, helping others is my favorite thing to do. And you may ask what's so good about it. Well, if I help someone else, then someone else will help me when I am in need. That's just the way it works. What goes around comes around."

"Shh, be quiet," said Chris. "She might hear you."

Vicky walked into the bank. She sat down across from the banker and talked with him as he explained what she was signing.

The banker said, "Have I answered all your questions?"

"Yes," replied Vicky.

"Okay, then I will need your signature in three places. I have them marked for you."

Vicky said, "Great, let me get my pen." She reached into her purse, removed Vick, and signed the papers.

The pen felt a little strange in her hand, she thought. She looked down and realized the refill was attached to the pen. With all the excitement of getting a new car, she overlooked the feel of the pen in her hand and signed the car loan papers.

Vick thought to himself, *This is so cool.*

Vicky laid Vick down on the desk.

Oh no, thought Vick, *I wonder if she will remember to pick me up and put me back in her purse?*

Vicky stood up, shook the banker's hand, and walked off without Vick.

Oh no, said Vick, *I am officially lost—no looking back now.*

Just then the Banker saw the pen. He lifted up Vick and said, "I can't remember if this was her pen or mine. Oh well." He put Vick in his cup holder with the other pens. The banker did not know that Vick was not just a regular Bick pen—he was a special pen.

All these pens look alike, thought Vick. *They are all engraved with the words "USA Bank."* He remained silent until the bank closed and everyone went home.

CHAPTER

10

VICK AND THE BANK PENS

Once it was silent and still in the bank, Vick introduced himself to the other pens in the cup. "Hi, my name is Vick, and I am a lost pen out on an adventure. I want to see the world."

There was an older, grumpy pen in the cup, whose ink was extremely low. He had signed all kinds of bank documents and had never left the bank. "Well, whoop-de-doo!" he said to Vick.

"I have been in this cup holder for years. No outside adventures ever occur at this bank. Everything happens in a very routine way. We are very conservative around here. So, chances are you will be in the cup holder with us for the rest of your life."

Vick said, "Well, I am going to think positively. I am not going to listen to your gloom and doom predictions. You know if you remain positive, wonderful things can happen. Being negative just blinds you from seeing all the opportunities that await you in this world. I bet I get out of here tomorrow."

"Well good luck with that!" replied the old pen.

Vick said, "It's been a great day. I got to see the inside of a bank and help someone get a new car by signing a car loan document. I can't wait to see what's next."

The grumpy pen replied, "Pipe down, kid; we are trying to sleep here. We have to get up early in the morning. We have banker's hours here. Our business is very serious—no clowning around."

Everyone went to sleep. Vick lay awake listening to all the other pens snore. *They are old,* he thought. *There is a lot of snoring going on here. I wonder what they do for fun?*

CHAPTER 11

WHERE IS VICK?

Meanwhile, back at Vicky's house, Bob had come over. Bob asked Vicky, "Have you used the pen yet?"

"Not yet, but let me go get it out of the drawer and put it in my purse right this minute." She had not realized that she had taken Vick to sign the car loan. She ran to the drawer and opened it. "Oh no!"

Bob shouted, "What's wrong?"

"Vick is gone! He's lost! I will never see him again!" shouted Vicky. She began to cry.

Bob said, "Don't worry. I will keep my eyes peeled. He is bound to turn up somewhere around here. He couldn't have left the house."

Vicky calmed down. "You are right. He has to be somewhere around the house. I will keep my eyes open as well. I guess crying over something that I have no control over is a waste of time. He is bound to show up eventually."

CHAPTER 12

THE BANK

The bank opened precisely at 9:00 a.m., and the first person through the door was a police officer named Pat. He was meeting with a banker to sign papers for a home loan. He was excited about getting his new house.

The banker greeted him and said, "Please step into my office."

Pat stepped inside.

The banker said, "Please meet our notary, Cindi. She will be verifying your signature today."

"Nice to meet you," said Pat.

The banker said, "There are four areas that will need your signature."

Pat reached for his pen that was supposed to be in his pocket. He kept one at all times because he never knew when he was going to have to write a traffic ticket. "That's funny; I guess I left my pen at home," he said.

Vick heard this and pushed himself up a little bit in the cup, so he could stand out. Of course, this occurred without anyone seeing him.

The banker said, "That is not a problem. You can use one of our pens. In fact, you can just keep it because I know you will need one for your job. Besides, you are a good customer. I see that you have been banking with us for years. I want you to have the pen as a way to say thank you for your business." The banker took a pen out of the cup—it was Vick.

The grumpy old pen said to the other pens, "Well, shut my mouth—he is going to get out of here. I guess having a positive attitude can get you somewhere."

The police officer signed the home loan papers and then put Vick in his shirt pocket.

Just as the policeman was getting ready to leave, a masked man entered the bank to rob it. He went up to the tellers and demanded cash.

The police officer, along with Vick, saw what was going on. He hid behind a bookcase to wait for an opportunity to catch the crook. He radioed for backup.

Vick thought, *Well today is going to be a real big adventure! I just hope I don't get shot. I could not survive a bullet.*

The robber ran out the door. Pat pulled out his gun and began chasing him. He yelled, "Stop! Police!" The robber kept running, so Pat ran faster. Vick was hanging on for dear life as he was thrown back and forth in Pat's shirt pocket.

The robber made it to his car. He jumped in and drove off.

Pat jumped into his police car and began chasing the man, his siren was blaring. He followed the man and radioed the location of the robber to the other policemen.

Eventually four police cars surrounded the robber, and he was forced to pull over to the side of the road, get out of his car, and surrender.

"Congratulations, Pat," said another police officer. "We would not have been able to capture this man if you had not been at the bank and pursued him. Great work! You showed him that crime does not pay!"

"Thanks—a raise would be nice since I just bought a new house," said Pat, laughing.

Pat then took out Vick and wrote up the necessary report to put the robber behind bars for a long time.

Wow, I just put a man behind bars, thought Vick. *Wait until all the supplies in Desk Drawer City hear about this adventure. Gosh, I sure wish I had a picture so they would believe me.*

At that very moment, a reporter stepped up to interview Pat. The reporter questioned Pat, and then said, "May I take a picture of you for the newspaper?"

"Sure," replied Pat.

Vick got his wish: a picture was taken of the police officer with Vick hanging out of his shirt pocket.

CHAPTER 13

THE DINER

The officer went to lunch at Butch's Diner. The waitress walked up to him to take his order and realized she did not have a pen. He said, "You can use mine."

Vick got to write out the policeman's lunch order and then the waitress gave the pen back to the officer.

Whew! That was close, thought Vick. *I would much rather be on an adventure with a policeman than writing food orders. I am glad she did not keep me. Besides writing all those orders would have used up a lot of my ink, and I am sure that I would not have made it out alive! It would be terrible to run out of ink and then be thrown away in the diner's trash. I would be mixed in with all those scraps of food. Now that would be a smelly ending.*

After lunch the policeman left the diner and got in his car. As fate would have it, a man sped by at that very moment. Pat started following him, his sirens on.

The driver of the car finally stopped. As Pat approached the vehicle, the man said, "I am so sorry, officer. I am a doctor, and I am on my way to deliver a baby at the hospital. It looks like the baby is coming sooner than expected."

"Well, I still am going to have to give you a ticket, but afterward I will give you a police escort to the hospital to help you get there quickly and safely. Rules are rules and are not meant to be broken. You could have killed someone back there. You were going way too fast."

"Yes, I understand," said the doctor.

Pat took out Vick and wrote up the speeding ticket. He handed the ticket, along with Vick, to the doctor so he could sign the necessary paperwork.

Just as the doctor was signing the ticket, his cell phone started to ring. He answered the call. A voice on the other line said, "Doctor, hurry up—the baby is coming soon!"

The doctor said to Pat, "I have to hurry! The baby is on the way." Without even a thought, he put Vick in his pocket. The policeman did not notice he had not received Vick back; he was too busy calling into the police station to let them know that he would be giving the doctor a police escort to the hospital.

CHAPTER 14

A BABY IS BORN

Boy, thought Vick, *now I understand how a pen can get lost. This is amazing! I am off to deliver a baby into the world! What a wonderful life I am leading.*

The doctor ran in the hospital with Vick still in his pocket. Vick didn't know what to expect, but he knew it was going to be fun!

The doctor quickly ran into a room to change into his scrubs. On his way into the delivery room, the doctor hung his clothes on a clothing rack in the adjoining room. Vick, still in the doctor's shirt pocket, could see through the glass that separated the rooms.

The baby was delivered very quickly and immediately began crying. Vick looked over at the parents and noticed that they were crying too. They were crying tears of joy! The event touched Vick so much that he got tears in his eyes.

How exciting, thought Vick. *This is unbelievable. No one will ever believe that I witnessed the birth of a child!*

The doctor went back into to the adjoining room to change back into the clothes that he had worn to the hospital. Of course, Vick was still in his pocket.

A couple of hours later, the doctor stopped by the room to check on the new mom, dad, and baby. A hospital staff person entered the room while the doctor was there. She told the parents, "I need you both to sign the birth certificate papers."

"We don't have a pen," they replied.

The doctor said, "I have a pen you can use." He took Vick out of his pocket and gave it to the dad. While the signing of the papers was happening, the doctor got paged to another room. He dashed out of the room and left Vick behind.

The hospital staff person gathered the signed papers and left Vick on the baby changing table in the room. *Oh, great,* thought Vick, *I am not sure what this table is used for, but I don't think it's going to be good.*

The baby began to cry. The dad lifted him up out of the crib and changed the baby's diaper right on that very table.

Vick got to smell a dirty diaper very up close. *Wow! This smell is awful! How can something so stinky come out of something so cute?* thought Vick.

Eventually the dad left to go home, and the baby and mom stayed at the hospital.

CHAPTER

VICK GOES TO WASHINGTON

The next morning rolled around and the dad stopped by the hospital to see his wife and new baby. It turned out that the dad was a senator. He said, "Honey, I hate to leave you, but I need to go to work today. I have to fly to Washington, because President Do-Right has asked me to be in his office when he signs a new bill into law. I was on the committee that submitted the law to the president. He has asked all committee members to be there for a picture that will be taken and submitted to the media." He leaned over and kissed his wife, who was holding the baby. He looked down and picked up Vick and asked, "If you don't mind, can I take this pen with me? I left mine at home."

"Of course, honey," said the mom. "I am not sure whose pen it is anyway. You can have it. Have a safe flight." The senator put Vick in his front shirt pocket.

How exciting! thought Vick. *I get to go to Washington and watch President Do-Right sign a bill. I am honored. I wonder how many pens actually get to see a president sign a bill into law? I hope a picture is taken. My friends will never believe it!*

The senator and Vick arrived a few minutes ahead of time to watch the president sign the bill. It was at the very moment they arrived that the president said, "I can't find my pen. Does anyone have one I can borrow?"

The Senator took Vick out of his pocket and said, "Sir, you can use mine."

President Do-Right used Vick Bick to sign the new bill into law. A picture was taken at the very moment Vick Bick was being used to sign the new bill into law. Vick was so excited to be in the picture. President Do-Right handed Vick Bick back to the senator.

The bill provided free ice cream sundaes for everyone on Sundays at all Dairy Doodle locations. *What an awesome bill! People everywhere will love this bill,* thought Vick. *I am glad I could be a part of something so wonderful.*

OVAL OFFICE

FREE
ICE CREAM

**President Do-Right Signs
Bill into Law**

CHAPTER 16

OUT OF THIS WORLD

Right after the picture was taken, a man entered the room, and President Do-Right said, "Gentlemen, I would like to introduce you to Glen John. He is an astronaut that will be going into space tomorrow. He will be exploring the moon."

Everyone clapped.

"I invited him here today to meet everyone and take a tour of the White House."

As the astronaut was leaving with the president for his White House tour, the senator leaned over and asked Glen John for his autograph. The senator said, "My son was just born, and your signature would make a wonderful baby gift." He handed the astronaut Vick Bick and a piece of paper for him to write on.

The astronaut signed the paper and was immediately distracted by other committee members wanting an autograph, so he used Vick for several more signatures. By the time the astronaut had finished signing autographs, the senator was gone. He had been called away to handle an important matter. The astronaut put the pen in his pocket. *I'll just have to mail it to him,* he thought.

Vick smiled as he thought about going to the moon. *How wonderful this is going to be. I wonder if my ink will be able to flow in space?* He patted the refill on his back and thought, *Good thing I have my ink refill with me. We could be there a long time.*

Finally, launch day for the rocket arrived. The astronaut put on his flight suit and stuck Vick in his pocket. He climbed into the rocket. About thirty minutes later, Vick heard the countdown and then "Blast off!" There was a loud explosion as the rocket headed for the sky!

When they finally made it into space, there was no gravity; Vick just floated around inside the rocket.

I am light as a feather! he thought. *Wow, I hope someone gets a picture of me with the astronaut.*

A couple of hours passed, and Vick found himself gazing out the window. He was looking at all the sparkling stars he saw in space. *What a beautiful scene,* he thought. Just then an explosion sounded, and a voice came over the intercom. It was someone from NASA.

"One of the engines just blew up. The explosion caused one of the fuel tanks to explode as well. You don't have enough fuel now to make it to the moon. We have to bring your ship back to Earth. There is a risk. There is a chance the rocket fuel runs out before you reach Earth, and you would crash."

The astronaut replied, "Okay, I understand," and then he bowed his head and prayed. "Dear Lord, please save me."

Vick thought, *All the supplies in Desk Drawer City warned me about getting lost if I left, but I never thought I could be lost in space!* Vick prayed as well. *God, please help us get home safely.*

Because of gravity's pull, Vick's refill cartridge flew off his back. *Oh no, I am in real trouble now! I only have a short amount of time left before I run out of ink!* he thought.

The scene in the rocket ship became one of great tension. The astronaut was obviously worried about not making it back alive, and Vick was worried about dying because of his lack of ink. What did the astronaut do to help relieve the stress of it all? He began playing country music!

Country music—well doesn't that beat all! thought Vick. *That would not have been my choice. At least he won't be able to hear me screaming as we plummet toward the Earth's atmosphere.*

As they fell rapidly toward Earth, Vick screamed. In between the screams, he would pray.

Finally, everything went black, and they hit the Atlantic Ocean near the Kennedy Space Center. Over the intercom a voice from NASA spoke: "Congratulations! Welcome home! You made it!" It wasn't too long before they were rescued from the floating spaceship.

CHAPTER

17

AT THE CHAPEL

Immediately after the astronaut was released from his briefing about the accident, he took Vick with him to church in Clearwater, Florida, to thank God for his safe landing. When they walked into the church, they saw the backs of a bride and groom. A wedding was getting ready to take place. They heard the preacher running up, shouting, "Quick—I need you both to sign this marriage certificate. The ceremony will start soon."

The groom and the bride turned around, and to Vick's surprise, it was Vicky and Bob! They were getting married. Vick was so excited. *This is great!* he thought. *I may have a chance to be saved after all.*

Bob and Vicky said, "We don't have a pen."

The pastor said, "Come to think of it, I don't either."

The astronaut said, "I have one you can use. As a matter of fact, you can keep it! Think of it as a wedding gift from me. You know this is a special pen; it went with me into space."

"Oh my, that's wonderful! Thank you so much!" said Vicky. As Vicky took the pen, she noticed the imprint on the side of the pen. "Oh my gosh, Bob—you aren't going believe it! It's Vick!"

Bob quickly moved closer to Vicky to gaze upon the pen. "That is Vick! How did you get into a space ship?"

Vick thought, *It is a long story! If only I could talk to them. Guess it will have to be one of those mysteries that they will have to ponder about for many years.*

The song "Here Comes the Bride" began to play. Bob put Vick in his shirt pocket and said, "It's showtime!"

Vick never dreamed that he would be Bob's best man in his wedding.

And in case you are wondering, there were a lot of pictures taken at the wedding, and yes, Vick was in all of them.

CHAPTER 18

THE HONEYMOON

Several hours passed, and then Vicky, Bob, and Vick were on a plane heading to the Caribbean for a honeymoon.

Vick thought, *A Caribbean vacation—now doesn't that beat it all. I do need to rest and relax after all these adventures that I have been through. The spaceship episode totally drained me!*

After they arrived, Vicky, Bob, and Vick went to the beach. Bob took Vick to help in filling out crossword puzzles.

Learning new words and how to spell is a lot of fun, thought Vick. *This could easily become my favorite new hobby.*

After seven days of being in the Caribbean, Bob, Vicky, and Vick returned home.

Vicky said, "Bob, I am going to put Vick in the desk drawer. I don't want him getting lost anymore."

Vicky ran upstairs, opened the desk drawer, and put Vick inside.

CHAPTER 19

THE HOMECOMING

Nighttime rolled around, and Bob and Vicky went to sleep. Everyone in the desk drawer woke up and began cheering!

"Welcome home, Vick!"

"We can't believe you made it back to Desk Drawer City! You are the first one we have known to make it back alive!"

"I am here for now, but I won't stay long. I was born to wander," said Vick. "But at least I made it back in time to get an ink refill. I was worried that I would run out of ink and be thrown away."

"It's time to celebrate!" said Mayor White Out.

Brigitte, the postcard, walked up to Vick and gave him a kiss. "I am so glad you are back. I wanted to mail myself to you several times, but I had no forwarding address."

A celebration was held that night in Vick's honor, and there was a lot of dancing going on. It was an awesome sight to see all the supplies dancing with each other. The rubber bands were the best dancers because of their flexibility.

Later that evening, Vick gave a presentation to everyone about what the outside world was like. He told them, "You know I won't be able to stay here very long. Soon I am going to want to get out of here again. It turns out that I was a misprint for a reason after all. Being different from all the other ink pens gave me the courage to go out into the world. I am proud to be different. I am proud to be Vick Bick. Soon I will need everyone's help again to get out of the drawer. We'll need a new plan."

Vick Bick began showing everyone the photo album of his adventures. As Vick turned the pages of the album, he explained where the pictures were taken. The photos included pictures of Vick in the policeman's pocket after catching the crook; Vick on a changing table in the hospital, holding his nose; Vick in space, floating around in the spaceship; Vick being held by President Do-Right as a new bill was signed into law; Vick pictured in Bob's pocket at Vicky and Bob's wedding; and Vick in the Caribbean, sitting in a lounge chair and wearing sunglasses.

Everyone laughed and had a good time, and when Max, the laptop computer, heard them, he became very irritated that Vick had made it back to the desk drawer. In anger, Max typed on his screen, "These supplies are useless. I'll have to think of a way to get rid of them soon."

It was at that very moment that Vicky entered the room and shut Max down.

ABOUT THE AUTHOR

Suzanne Coffey Mielke was born in Tennessee. Her father, Charlie Coffey, was a college football coach, and the family lived in Florida, Louisiana, Washington, DC, Tennessee, Arkansas, and Virginia during his coaching career. She graduated from the University of Tennessee, with a major in fashion merchandising. Her career profile has included retail management and buying, owning her own catering company, and conducting radio sales, with the majority of her career (seventeen years) spent as an executive television producer. She is the mother of two grown children, who are married, and the grandmother of six grandchildren, who refer to her as Zuzu. Suzanne is the author of another book entitled *Providence Road*. Suzanne is presently living in Charlotte, North Carolina.

CPSIA information can be obtained
at www.ICGtesting.com
Printed in the USA
BVHW052028150720
583811BV00004B/195

9 781489 729514